The Mechanical Chess Invention

Published and distributed by:
Voices of Future Generations International Children's Book Series
Trust for Sustainable Living
Hampstead Norreys, Berkshire, RG18 0TN, United Kingdom
Tel: +44 (0)1635 202444
Web: www.vofg.org

Special thanks to René V. Steiner for layout and graphics support:
www.steinergraphics.com.

The Voices of Future Generations International Children's Book Series:
'The Epic Eco-Inventions' by Jona David (Europe/North America), illustrated by Carol Adlam
'The Great Green Vine Invention' by Jona David (Europe/North America), illustrated by Carol Adlam
'The Tree of Hope' by Kehkashan Basu (Middle East), illustrated by Karen Webb-Meek
'The Fireflies After the Typhoon' by Anna Kuo (Asia), illustrated by Siri Vinter
'The Species-Saving Time Team' by Lautaro Real (Latin America), illustrated by Dan Ungureanu
'The Sisters' Mind Connection' by Allison Lievano-Gomez (Latin America), illustrated by Oscar Pinto
'The Forward and Backward City' by Diwa Boateng (Africa), illustrated by Meryl Treatner
'The Voice of an Island' by Lupe Vaai (Pacific Islands), illustrated by Li-Wen Chu
'The Visible Girls' by Tyronah Sioni (Pacific Islands), illustrated by Kasia Nieżywińska
'The Mechanical Chess Invention' by Jona David (Europe/North America), illustrated by Dan Ungureanu

Under the patronage of
UNESCO

United Nations
Educational, Scientific and
Cultural Organization

The Mechanical Chess Invention

by
Jona David

Illustrated by Dan Ungureanu

foreword

Jona David, Laureate of our Human Rights Commission's first-ever Justitia Regnorum Junior Award, is a creative, courageous and serious boy who works hard to overcome challenges and is passionately committed to the rights of future generations. His awareness-raising and environmental education efforts, as the European / North American Child Author in the United Nations Voices of Future Generations Children's Initiative, have reached thousands of children around the world. He shows dedication, imagination and insight beyond his years, in his call for children to speak up for what they believe in, to stand up for each other and our Earth, and to find creative solutions to our social and environmental problems by working together.

This book is a creative, courageous and caring insight into the troubles and triumphs of a child's world. The story of two brothers and their friends who uncover a dastardly plot to take over the world and find a whimsical way to win through, is classic Jona David. It is a pleasure to recommend this book to all readers, young and old, and to know that our future is in good hands with children like Jona.

Professor Marcel Szabo
Chair, Voices of Future Generations Children's Initiative &
Commissioner for Future Generations, Hungary

preface

Chess is known as the Game of Kings. In Jona David's story, however, chess also becomes an unlikely saviour of the world and an insightful challenge to the fads and fashions of our society.

Jona and his own little brother Nico, like the children in this story, are both avid chess players, who have represented the Cambridgeshire schools' chess team.

This volume, written by a young pupil to honour the forty years of service of the the Chess teacher and former Head of History of King's College School, Cambridge, Mr Robert Henderson (Hendy), is a testament to the respect, intellectual agility and imagination celebrated in a game which Voltaire described as 'the game which confers most honour on human wit'.

It is a pleasure to commend this adventure story to readers young and old.

Nicholas Jackson & Robert Henderson
Cambridgeshire Chess League
www.chessforkids.co.uk

chapter 1

In a house on a lake in a very green town, lived a boy and his Little Brother .The boy was a Mad Genius Eco-Inventor, and his joyful Little Brother helped to share his inventions around the world. They had many cool adventures together.

The two boys studied in a Terribly Good School, and it was the start of term. They were going to the school library to submit their entries for the school's Creativity Prize. The Eco-Inventor Boy carried his secret entry in a large box that made clanking noises. His Little Brother had painted endangered species posters.

As they walked through the school, they saw a big group of older boys around a tabletop, shouting and pushing. The Little Brother tried to get closer to see what they were playing, but he was rudely shoved away.

"What is going on?" he asked his brother. "Oh," said the Eco-Inventor Boy. "It is a very odd phenomenon. They are making battles between little plastic spinning war robots – they call them Spinners."

"Why are they using such ugly plastic toys?" asked the Little Brother, who was very friendly and joyful and not used to being pushed.

"It is the latest fad," answered the Eco-Inventor Boy. "It has caught on really fast. I find it all a bit suspicious. No one even knows where they came from. But suddenly, everyone wants one. The kids think it will make them more popular."

The brothers politely gave their prize entries to the kind and gentle Terribly Good Librarian. Then, they headed home.

While the Eco-Inventor Boy was practicing with his brilliant chess tutor, the Little Brother slipped into the cupboard under the stairs with his robot spider friend, who could turn invisible and had been a gift from his older brother.

By following an underground tunnel, they soon came to the Eco-Inventor Boy's Secret Laboratory under the island in their lake.

As usual, they found lots of scientific equipment and half-built inventions. A caretaker robot was cleaning the walls. A new series of mechanical undersea animals were busily building a nano-habitat of a giant coral reef.

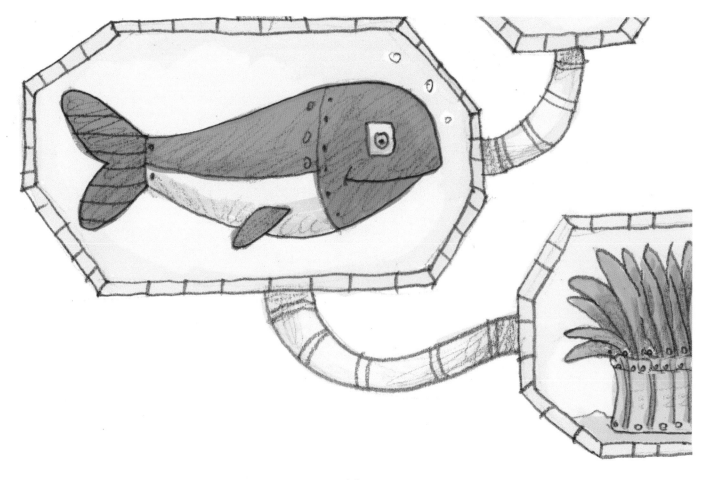

The friends jumped onto the anti-gravity trampoline, laughing together. But they accidentally triggered a special lever. The bouncy part suddenly dropped and they floated downwards. They were amazed – they never knew the Secret Laboratory had a hidden cellar!

"This must be his Sub-Level 2!" said the Little Brother, and his robot spider chirped in agreement. Deep underground, the Sub-Level 2 Lab focused on mechanical inventions.

A huge workbench ran along one wall, and there was a big flat worktable. Special drawers and boxes were full of all kinds of strange mechanical and electric tools like robot screwdrivers, magnetised hammers, winged wrenches, diamond saws, magma mini-drills, a soldering iron that could solder anything eight-at-once, moulds for shaping materials with special properties, a polymer and molymer combining machine, and even a special particle-proof chamber to construct robots in vacuum.

He recognised one thing on the worktable right away: it was a Chess Set. But all the metal pieces were mechanised and moving! "This must be my brother's Secret Entry for the Creativity Prize," he said in awe. Before they returned through the secret tunnel for tea, they noted a couple of really amazing inventions.

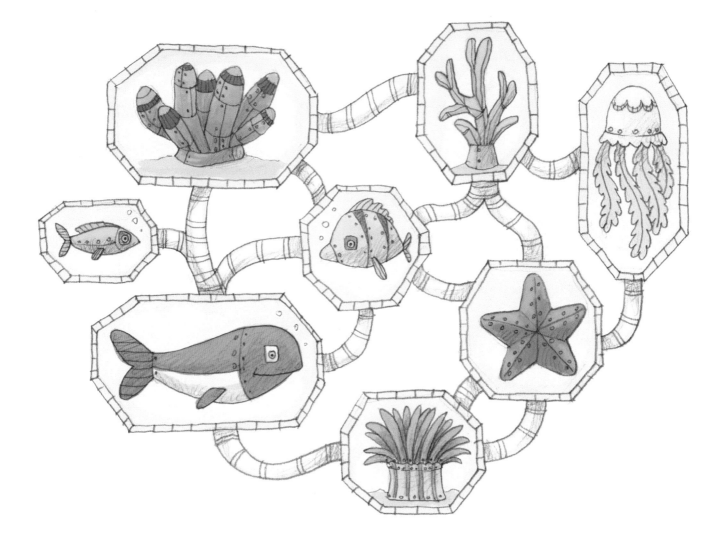

There were undersea mechanical toys of endangered species, which could build their own coral reef nano-habitats.

UNDERSEA CORAL REEF NANO-ZOO

1. Force-fields for coral reef undersea habitats and retaining seawater
2. Nano-tech frames and tiny coloured marbles for building ocean-habitats inside globes
3. Basic positronic units for learning swimming, flipping and habitat-building skills
4. Special anti-rust plating for underwater mechanical parts

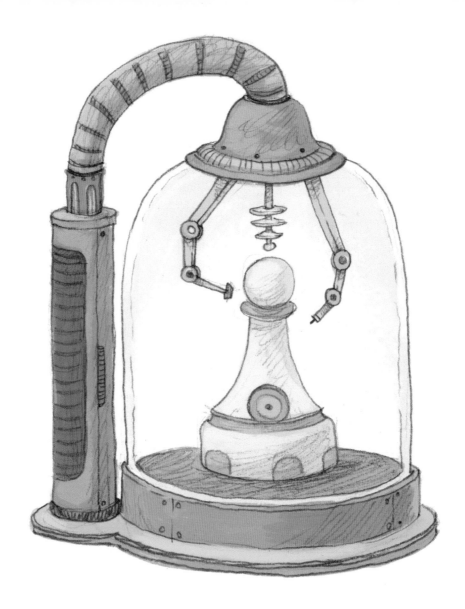

There was a special robo-assembler with a particle-proof chamber to construct robots in a vacuum.

ROBO-ASSEMBLER WITH VACUUM CHAMBER

1. Vacuum pump that removes air and all particles from robot assembly chamber
2. Smart robotic arms with tiny assembly tools and 360 degree rotating hinges
3. Shatter-proof reinforced glass backed by force fields to keep vacuum environment intact
4. Advanced positronic units for applying robot-creation and construction skills

chapter 2

The next day, at the Terribly Good School, a friend of the Little Brother found him. The friend was deaf and had helped in other adventures. She was carrying a plastic spinner with a tiny broken nozzle poking out. She looked worried. She had a strange rash on her hand. "Maybe your inventor brother should investigate these things," said the deaf girl, in sign language.

Back in his Sub-Level 2 Lab, the Eco-Inventor Boy dissected the broken spinner. He found some very odd things. It seemed like only a plastic toy. But it had a hollow chamber leading to many spinning retractable spray-nozzles.

Curiously, the broken spinner had no obvious source of power, just a tiny satellite dish on its main body.

Also, there was a mysterious computer chip at the centre where the robot brain should be, almost like the spinner was meant to be activated and controlled from a distance!

"This is more than just a little toy," declared the Eco-Inventor Boy. "But like any fad, it is taking over. There must be thousands of these things in schools and homes all over the country, by this time. What kind of power source could be used to activate them with a satellite dish? And why?"

Two levels up and on the shore, in the boys' lakehouse, the doorbell rang. The Little Brother and his robot spider pet answered.

But instead of a person, on the doorstep was the long, leafy arm of a Great Green Vine. And it beckoned frantically!

The Little Brother immediately sent his robot spider to get the Eco-Inventor Boy.

The vine tugged the Eco-Inventor Boy, and all the children rushed to the forest across the lake. In one of their adventures, they had set a nebula gas fuel cell into an iron lantern tree, to keep the Great Green Vine company at nighttimes.

They arrived at the great green forest and made their way to the tree. They saw immediately why the vine was so panicked. The nebula gas fuel cell was normally shining brightly with indigo-blue light. But now, the lantern tree was dark and silent. The fuel cell was gone. It had been stolen!

Beside the empty lantern, a note had been left in a dirty plastic pop bottle. It read, "My Evul Plan To Take Over The World Has Begun. And Your Fuwel Cell Invenshun Will Be Very Useful!"

The Eco-Inventor Boy looked grimly at the sky. "It seems," he said in a calm voice, "that I have a nemesis. And he has bad spelling."

chapter 3

The two boys and their pet robot spider returned to the Sub-Level 2 Laboratory under the lake.

The Eco-Inventor Boy took the note over to a side table where he kept his scanners. He discovered a strange symbol on the back. It looked like a spiral reverse question mark with devil horns.

He was sure he'd seen it before somewhere. As he worked, the pet robot spider poked at the half-dissected plastic spinner. It broke. And on the back of the tiny disk was the same spiral reverse question mark with horns!

"The maker of these spinners must be the same Evil Inventor who has stolen my nebula gas fuel cell!" said the Inventor Boy. "And that means, the spinners are part of his plan to take over the world!"

The Little Brother gasped. "Oh no!" he cried. "We must stop him! But what can we do?" The Inventor Boy quickly did some internet research.

They searched for the spinners online, and the reverse question mark immediately popped up, on the website at www.EvilInventor.com!

My Evul Plan to Take Over the Werld

On the homepage, children were encouraged to use their parents' credit cards to buy spinners. A Manifesto popped up, entitled "My Evul Plan to Take Over the World."

The website pretended to be only selling spinners, but perhaps the goal of the manifesto was real. They could see from the blueprints that spinners were meant to be remote controlled. Using power from the nebula gas fuel cell, they could be activated as an army, their mechanical arms spraying poisonous chemicals to eliminate all living creatures.

"We have to stop them!" cried the Little Brother.

"Don't worry," said the Eco-Inventor Boy with discipline and determination, "The toxic chemicals won't win. We will stop them. But I need to run some tests."

The Little Brother and his robot spider dashed back to their Terribly Good School, to try and collect more of the suspicious spinners.

When they got to school, they heard shouting. "Hello? Hello? Someone let us out of here!!!" The voice was coming from a broom closet in the school cellar. The robot spider quickly tricked the closet lock.

Three of the older popular children had been kept captive for a long time. But they were the same kids who had been handing out spinners to everyone!

The Little Brother realized immediately that the big kids must have been locked up and replaced by evil clones. "When I got shoved," he said to his big buddy, "it wasn't really you at all!"

They all agreed that the Evil Plan had to be stopped. Just then, the Eco-Inventor Boy arrived, pulling a wagon full of mechanical objects that clanked.

chapter 4

"I am so glad that you are here! Do you have a solution?" asked the Little Brother. "I think I might," replied the Eco-Inventor Boy. "Oh good! What a relief!" exclaimed the Little Brother. "I was so worried."

The older boys were worried too. "There must be thousands of these spinners at ready, all across the country! How can we possibly stop them all?"

"That is indeed the challenge. I have to think of something every house and school needs. A gift that we can send people, to fight the spinners," explained the Eco-Inventor Boy. "And I know exactly what might work… a chess set!"

"How could chess help to fight the invasion of the spinner fad?" asked the older boys. "Well, this is not exactly an ordinary chess set," answered the Inventor Boy. "It is my Mechanical Chess Invention. I made some rather special modifications."

He pulled the cover off his wagon, and two Chess Rooks immediately hovered at attention, using their mechanical jet engines.

MECHANICAL CHESS SET

1. Pesticide-proof steel plating to protect chess pieces from dangerous chemicals
2. Tiny mechanical jet engines and sonic booms for mobility, powered by nebula gas fuel cells
3. Miniature laser spears, electrified chain-saw swords and shields, comet-shooting cannons, lightning conducting long staffs, crowns that project electrical fire rings and mirrors to channel light weapons
4. Antidote sprays to neutralize dangerous chemicals

STRICTLY CONFIDENTIAL

"This is your Creativity Prize entry," said the Little Brother. "Can it stop those horrible spinners from spraying chemicals everywhere and poisoning all living things?"

The Inventor Boy smiled. "I have given each piece pesticide-proof steel plating and the Kings have antidote sprays. But they will have to defeat the spinners to win." He took the prototype Mechanical Chess Set out of his wagon and set it up in the school hall with his Duplicator Machine. "We will have to get them to people quickly," said the older boys. "We'll all help with that. It is the least we can do."

In a few hours, children all around the country were receiving new chess sets in their schools and homes.

Everyone was delighted. They had no idea that their spinners were dangerous, or that their chess sets might be just a little… unusual.

The Inventor Boy and his Little Brother knew from the 'Evul Plan to Take Over the World' website that the spinner activation would happen on Tuesday at 2pm, when many children were in school and could be easily locked up.

Sure enough, the next day was Tuesday, and, at 2pm, the Evil Inventor began laughing crazily. He activated the nebula gas fuel cell to energize his plastic robots by remote control.

Across the country, thousands and thousands of spinners grew long, sharp, wiry legs and platinum claws. Their poisonous spray-pipe nozzles shot up. They took note of their environments and the closest living creatures. Controlled by the mini satellite dishes on their bodies, they began to whirl forward for their invasion.

chapter 5

In the next few seconds, in all the schools and homes across the country, the Mechanical Chess Invention sprang into defensive action. First, the Mechanical Pawns marched out, beaming laser spears which cut through the legs of the spinners, knocking them to the ground and melting their poison nozzles.

Then, the Mechanical Knights whipped out their electrical chain-saw swords and shields and used sonic booms to leap forwards and sideways over obstacles, and slicing the spinners in half. The spinners started spraying their toxic pesticides and shot out wires to catch the brave Chess defenders.

But the Mechanical Rooks simply cleared down the files, shooting comets from tiny cannons to explode each spinner where it stood. As the spinners regrouped and whirled forward to attack, the Mechanical Bishops went into action across the diagonals, slicing lightning from long staffs and frying the spinners satellite brains.

Unfortunately, there were thousands of spinners and they threatened to overwhelm the Mechanical Chess Sets in sheer numbers. But fortunately, the Mechanical Queens were brought out, with a sweeping ring of electrical fire in all directions, melting the spinners into lumps of helpless plastic. Before long, it was nearly all over, and the Kings and Rooks were already cornering the last few spinners in the end game.

Everyone cheered as the last half-melted spinners were dosed with antidotes by the Kings, which made them harmless. The plastic was converted into recycled parts for school playground sets. The Mechanical Chess Sets bowed and then marched away in triumph. The Evil Inventor had been foiled.

The Eco-Inventor Boy and his Little Brother knew that it was not over. The Evil Inventor was still out there with the stolen nebula gas fuel cell. He would surely be back.

Still, together with their friends as well as all teachers at the Terribly Good School, and all the schools and homes across the country, they had many celebrations.

At the Creativity Prize awards ceremony, the Inventor Boy even won the second place Creativity Prize for his Mechanical Chess Invention! He went up to shake their wise Headmaster's hand, then happily joined their first place deaf friend, who had written a beautiful symphony using only maths equations. And the Little Brother won a pre-prep Prize for his endangered species posters.

Everyone decided not to buy anything just because of a silly fad again. Indeed, they started a special class to learn about sustainability values at each school, instead. Thousands of children also joined school chess clubs. They now understood the true brilliance of the game.

The End (for now)

about the author

Jona David is a 11 year old boy from King's College School, Cambridge, and a prize-winning child author. He participated in the 2012 United Nations Conference on Sustainable Development in Rio de Janeiro and serves as a United Nations Child Ambassador for the Sustainable Development Goals. He won the 2016 Justitia Regnorum Fundamentum Junior Award for his work on children's environmental rights, 2nd place worldwide in the Trust for Sustainable Living International Essay Competition in 2015 in Oxford and in 2016 in Dubai, also the KCS Global Education Prize, and Gold in the UK Primary and Junior Maths Competition, and he helps lead his school's Eco-Society. His stories have been published in The Guardian, and in the UN Voices of Future Generations Children's Book Series. Jona enjoys maths and science, especially physics, biology, chemistry and space, chess, reading, canoeing, aikido and polo. He loves creating blueprints for eco-inventions and writing about them, but it will take a while to learn how to build them. He thanks his mother, father and little brother Nico for all their help and inspiration.

about the illustrator

Dan Ungureanu has always loved drawing. As he preferred colour pencils to any toy in his early childhood, his parents decided to arrange painting lessons for him, so before learning to read he was taught to draw.

He studied painting in Romania and started working in different artistic fields, such as graphic design, concept art, story-boarding for animation movies, and painting. In 2010, he had the chance to illustrate a poem book for children and realized that this is the main path that he wants to follow. A couple of other book projects have reached his desk since then, and with each project he has learned something new.

In 2013, he decided to join the MA in Children's Book Illustration at the Cambridge School of Art, feeling the need to understand and learn more about the subject. He says this was one of his best decisions and that his main achievement in course work was gaining the confidence to not just illustrate but also write his own stories for children.

Voices of Future Generations Children's Book Series

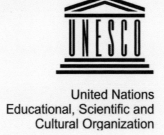
United Nations
Educational, Scientific and
Cultural Organization

Under the patronage of
UNESCO

The United Nations Convention on the Rights of the Child

All children are holders of important human rights. Twenty-five years ago in 1989, over a hundred countries agreed a UN Convention on the Rights of the Child. In the most important human rights treaty in history, they promised to protect and promote all children's equal rights, which are connected and equally important.

In the 54 Articles of the Convention, countries make solemn promises to defend children's needs and dreams. They recognize the role of children in realizing their rights, being heard and involved in decisions. Especially, Article 24 and Article 27 defend children's rights to safe drinking water, good food, a clean and safe environment, health, quality of life. And Article 29 recognizes children's rights to education that develops personality, talents and potential, respecting human rights and the natural environment.

— *Dr. Alexandra Wandel*
World Future Council

Voices of Future Generations Children's Book Series

United Nations
Educational, Scientific and
Cultural Organization

Under the patronage of
UNESCO

The UN Sustainable Development Goals

At the United Nations Rio+20 Conference on Sustainable Development in 2012, governments and people came together to find pathways for a safer, more fair, and greener world for all. Everyone agreed to take new action to end poverty, stop environmental problems, and build bridges to a more just future. In 283 paragraphs of *The Future We Want* Declaration, countries committed to defend human rights, steward resources, fight climate change and pollution, protect animals, plants and biodiversity, and look after oceans, mountains, wetlands and other special places.

In the United Nations, countries are committing to 17 new Sustainable Development Goals for the whole world, with targets for real actions on the ground. Clubs, governments, firms, schools and children have started over a thousand partnerships, and mobilized billions, to deliver. The future we want exists in the hearts and minds of our generation, and in the hands of us all.

— Vuyelwa Kuuya
Centre for International Sustainable Development Law (CISDL)

Voices of Future Generations Children's Book Series

Under the patronage of
UNESCO

United Nations
Educational, Scientific and
Cultural Organization

Thanks and Inspiring Resources

'Voices of Future Generations' International Commission
Warmest thanks to the International Commission, launched in 2014 by His Excellency Judge CG Weeramantry, UNESCO Peace Education Research Award Laureate, which supports, guides and profiles this new series of Children's Books Series, including Ms Alexandra Wandel (WFC), Dr Marie-Claire Cordonier Segger (CISDL), Dr Kristiann Allen (New Zealand), Ms Irina Bokova (UNESCO), Mr Karl Hansen (Trust for Sustainable Living), Ms Emma Hopkin (UK), Dr Ying-Shih Hsieh (EQPF), Dr Maria Leichner-Reynal (Uruguay), Ms Melinda Manuel (PNG), Ms Julia Marton-Lefevre (IUCN), Dr James Moody (Australia), Ms Anna Oposa (The Philippines), Professor Kirsten Sandberg (UN CRC Chair), Ms Patricia Chaves (UN DSD), Dr Marcel Szabo (Hungary), Dr Christina Voigt (Norway), Ms Gabrielle Sacconaghi-Bacon (Moore Foundation), Ms Marcela Orvañanos de Rovzar (UNICEF Mexico) and others.

The World Future Council consists of 50 eminent global changemakers from across the globe. Together, they work to pass on a healthy planet and just societies to our children and grandchildren. (www.worldfuturecouncil. org)

United Nations Education, Science and Culture Organization (UNESCO) which celebrates its 70th Anniversary throughout 2015, strives to build networks among nations that enable humanity's moral and intellectual solidarity by mobilizing for education, building intercultural understanding, pursuing scientific cooperation, and protecting freedom of expression. (en.unesco.org)

The **United Nations Committee on the Rights of the Child (CRC)** is the body of 18 independent experts that monitors implementation of the Convention on the Rights of the Child, and its three Optional Protocols, by its State parties. (www.ohchr.org)

United Nations Environment Programme (UNEP) provides leadership and encourages partnership in caring for the environment by inspiring, informing, and enabling nations and peoples to improve their quality of life without compromising that of future generations. (www.unep.org)

International Union for the Conservation of Nature (IUCN) envisions a just world that values and conserves nature, working to conserve the integrity and diversity of nature and to ensure that any use of natural resources is equitable and ecologically sustainable. (www.iucn.org)

Centre for International Sustainable Development Law (CISDL) supports understanding, development and implementation of law for sustainable development by leading legal research through scholarship and dialogue, and facilitating legal education through teaching and capacity-building. (www.cisdl.org)

Trust for Sustainable Living and its Living Rainforest Centre exist to further the understanding of sustainable living in the United Kingdom and abroad through high-quality education. (www.livingrainforest.org)

Environmental Quality Protection Foundation (EQPF) established in 1984 is the premier ENGO in Taiwan. Implementing environmental education, tree plantation, and international participation through coordinating transdisciplinarity resources to push forward environmental and sustainable development in our time.

Voices of Future Generations Children's Book Series

Under the patronage of
UNESCO

United Nations
Educational, Scientific and
Cultural Organization

About the 'Voices of Future Generations' Series

To celebrate the 25th Anniversary of the United Nations Convention on the Rights of the Child, the Voices of Future Generations Children's Book Series, led by the United Nations and a consortium of educational charities including the World Future Council (WFC), the Centre for International Sustainable Development Law (CISDL), the Environmental Quality Protection Foundation (EQPF), the Fundacion Ecos and the Trust for Sustainable Living (TSL) among others, also the Future Generations Commissioners of several countries, and international leaders from the UN Division for Sustainable Development, the UN Committee on the Rights of the Child, the UN Education, Science and Culture Organisation (UNESCO), the International Union for the Conservation of Nature (IUCN), and other international organizations, has launched the new Voices of Future Generations Series of Children's Books.

Every year we feature stories from our selected group of child authors, inspired by the outcomes of the Earth Summit, the Rio+20 United Nations Conference on Sustainable Development (UNCSD) and the world's Sustainable Development Goals, and by the Convention on the Rights of the Child (CRC) itself. Our junior authors, ages 8-12, are concerned about future justice, poverty, the global environment, education and children's rights. Accompanied by illustrations, each book profiles creative, interesting and adventurous ideas for creating a just and greener future, in the context of children's interests and lives.

We aim to publish the books internationally in ten languages, raising the voices of future generations and spread their messages for a fair and sustainable tomorrow among their peers and adults, worldwide. We welcome you to join us in support of this inspiring partnership, at www.vofg.org.

13795628R00034

Printed in Germany
by Amazon Distribution
GmbH, Leipzig